Use these stickers for the activities in the book

Page 2

Pages 2–3

Here's a mouse!

Here's a mouse!

Here's a mouse!

Page 16

Why must you go?

I forgot the time!

Page 18

Page 20

Page 14

ere | air | ear | are

Page 17

j | J | g | g

Page 21

c | k

Page 4

b
b | b | b | b

Page 7

w | w
w | w

Page 8

ng | ng
ng | ng

Page 11

a | a | a
a | a

Page 13

cl | cl
gl | gl

Page 22

nd | nd
nd | nd

Page 24

Cinderella
near | clap
wing | glass
patch | just
magic | kind

Treat yourself to a gold star for trying the activities!

Well done! (×12)

Reading Together
Cinderella

Phonics Consultant: Susan Purcell
Illustrator: Giuliana Gregori
Concept: Fran Bromage

Miles
Kelly

Read aloud focusing on the s sound (as in silly)

Once upon a time, there was a girl called Cinderella, who often felt sad.

She had two silly stepsisters, and a stepmother who was not very nice to her.

Use your arrow stickers to point to three mice.

Say the names as you spot each person.

Stick on their stickers.

Cinderella

sister

sister

Cinderella worked hard, but the sisters were never satisfied. Every night Cinderella sat by the fireside with the mice.

What a good try! Put a gold star here.

Sound out these words with the s sound.

ice   saucer   set   sell

circus   city   ceiling

3

... on the b
...und (as in ball)
as you read
aloud

One day the two stepsisters were being beastly to Cinderella, when a letter arrived.

It was an invitation to a ball at the palace, but Cinderella's stepmother banned her from going.

Use your stickers to **spell** some words beginning with b.

bake   box   bear   bird   bulb

Instead, Cinderella had to help both her bossy sisters get ready for the ball.

"We look fabulous," they boasted.

Say the names of the things in the pictures as you find them. They all use the b sound.

bows   beads   ribbons

bucket   basket

I don't want to stay h**ere**.

As the carriage disapp**ear**ed, Cinderella felt t**ear**s come to her eyes.

The palace was so n**ear**, but Cinderella f**ear**ed she would never see inside it.

Sound out these words with the **ear** sound.

year   clear   beard
cheer   steer   deer

6

Suddenly, an old woman with glittery wings and a wand appeared!

"I'm your fairy godmother!" she said with a wave of her wand. "You will have your wish and go to the ball!"

"First, we will need to find some things," she said, with a wink.

Use your stickers to **spell** some words beginning with **w**.

week   wash   wool   winter

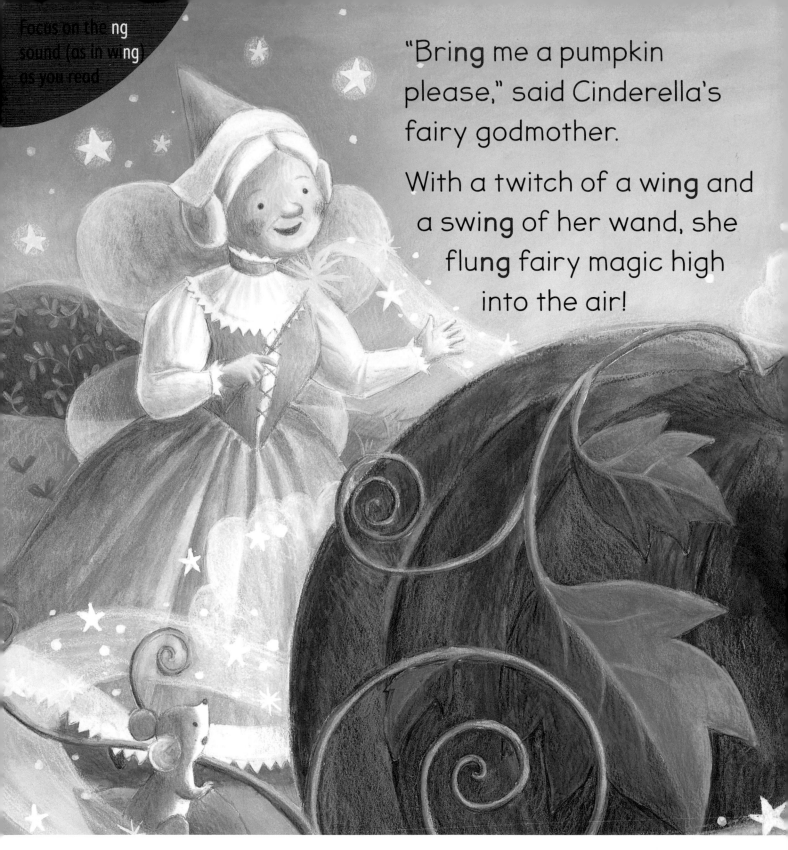

"Bring me a pumpkin please," said Cinderella's fairy godmother.

With a twitch of a wing and a swing of her wand, she flung fairy magic high into the air!

Use your stickers to **spell** some words with the ng sound.

king   thing   young   along

8

A big, ripe pumpkin from the vegetable patch grew so big it looked as if it was ready to pop!

Sound out these words with the **p** sound in different positions.

park   poster   paper   puppy

chip   sheep   cheap

Draw attention to the or sound (as in horse)

The enormous pumpkin transformed into a beautiful carriage, while four mice became stunning white horses!

Sound out these words with the **or** sound.

fork   corn   born   sport

short   pour   your

As the magic swirled around, a brown rat turned into a coachman and Cinderella clapped her hands.

Use your stickers to **spell** some words, which all use the **a** sound.

map   flag   ant   add   apple

With a **cl**ap of her hands, Cinderella's **cl**ever fairy godmother turned Cinderella's plain **cl**othes into a **gl**amorous gown.

Cinderella's hair became **gl**ossy, and on her feet were **gl**ittery **gl**ass slippers.

Sound out these words beginning with the cl and gl blends.

cloud   click   class   club

glove   glad   glue

12

Cinderella **glowed** with happiness.

"Keep a **close** eye on the **clock**," warned the fairy godmother. "The spell will end when the **clock** strikes twelve."

Use your stickers to **spell** some more words beginning with the **cl** and **gl** blends.

climb   **cliff**   **glow**   **glare**

Emphasize
the air sound
(as in hair)

As Cinderella arrived at the palace,
wearing her stunning gown and with jewels
in her hair, everyone turned to stare.
"Who is that fair lady?" asked the prince.

Cinderella's stepsisters
didn't recognize her, but they
glared as she walked down the stairs.

Use your stickers to **spell** some words with the **air** sound.

there   chair   bear   share

14

The prince spun Cinderella into the middle of the room.

They danced all night by the light of the moon.

The prince felt he had found his true love.

Sound out these words with the **oo** sound.

spoon   zoo   blue   glue

chew   threw

15

Highlight the ie sound (as in tie)

While the dancing carried on into the night, the clock struck twelve.

Cinderella gave a frightened cry – she hadn't noticed the time!"

Stick on the speech bubbles with the ie sound.

As she ran down the flight of steps she left behind a glass slipper.

Sound out some words with the **ie** sound.

mine   smile   wild   find

tie   pie   try   by   might

Cinderella jumped into the carriage, but the magic wore off just as she started the journey home.

The carriage turned back into a **g**iant pumpkin, the horses became mice and her gown and jewels vanished.

Use your stickers to **spell** some words with the j sound.

jug   **j**elly   **g**entle   **g**iraffe

The handsome prince's heart was heavy. He had fallen in love with Cinderella, and wanted to visit every house in his country with her glass slipper.

Say the words as you spot things with the h sound.

Stick on their stickers.

18

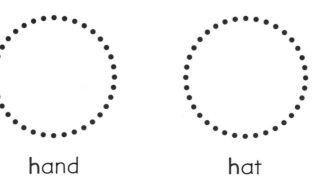

hand   hat   hair

"I will **h**unt **h**igh and low," said the prince. "**Wh**oever this slipper fits shall be my bride."

Soon **h**e arrived at Cinderella's **h**ome.

Sound out these words with the **h** sound.

hill   **help**   **hold**   **hurry**

whose   **whole**

The prince called everyone in to try on the slipper. Of course, the stepsisters' feet couldn't fit.

Cinderella stood quietly in the corner. "Can you try it too?" asked the prince.

Say the words as you spot things with the k sound.

Stick on their stickers.

20

cushion

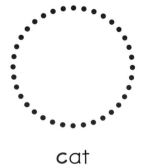

cat

candle

"She can't try it on, she works in the kitchen," replied Cinderella's cunning stepmother.

The kind prince lifted Cinderella's foot onto the cushion. The slipper fitted! No one could believe it.

Use your stickers to **complete** the sentence with the **k** sound.

"She can't try it on, she works in the kitchen."

"I've found you!" said the kind prince. He took Cinderella's hand in his, and asked her to marry him.

Her stepsisters could only stand by and watch as the prince and Cinderella became husband and wife.

Use your stickers to **spell** some words ending with the **nd** blend.

se**nd**   ba**nd**   mi**nd**   po**nd**

22

Ask your child to **retell** the story using
these key sounds and story images.

Cinderella   bossy   wish

horses   stare   room

cry   hunt   husband

Use your stickers to **add** a word that matches
the red highlighted **sounds** on each line.

set   city   saucer   [   ]

cheer   beard   deer

bring   young   along

pumpkin   chip   pop

map   hand   add

cloud   click   clock

glad   glove   glossy

jug   gentle   giraffe

cat   kitchen   candle

24

You've had fun with phonics! Well done.